JUST

BEFORE

DAYBREAK

*a life lived
between yesterday
and tomorrow*

DEANNA LOREA

THOUGHT
CATALOG
Books

THOUGHTCATALOG.COM

Copyright © 2025 Deanna Lorea.

All rights reserved. No part of this book may be reproduced or transmitted in any form or any means, electronic or mechanical, without prior written consent and permission from Thought Catalog.

Published by Thought Catalog Books®, an imprint of Thought Catalog, a digital magazine owned and operated by The Thought & Expression Co. Inc., an independent media organization founded in 2010 and based in the United States of America. For stocking inquiries, contact stockists@shopcatalog.com.

Produced by Chris Lavergne and Noelle Beams
Art direction and design by KJ Parish
Circulation management by Isidoros Karamitopoulos
Author biography written by Vaughn W. Hebron

thoughtcatalog.com | shopcatalog.com

First Limited Edition Print
Printed in the United States of America

ISBN 978-1-965820-22-3

TABLE OF CONTENTS

PREFACE
11

PART 1

SUDDENLY

15

PART 2

FINALLY

129

When you come to the end of self,
all that survives, all that matters, is unveiled.

—DEANNA LOREA

"The pain of staying here will be worse than the pain of starting over…"

JUST BEFORE DAYBREAK

Sometimes you need to take a few steps *back* in order to take more steps forward.

PREFACE

I couldn't have predicted this arrival on my best day...

It's cold. And not in the sense of temperature, but in the sense of departure. Something has left me and in its void, I feel cold. Just days ago I was planning for a new baby, dreaming of expanding life with a partner who departed without a goodbye less than an hour ago. It was a small fight. I left the house to breathe through the frustration and returned to an empty home. No sign of him anywhere. No shoes left by the door, no clothes hanging in the closet. No razor left on the bathroom counter. He left. How do you go from planning a future in your womb to barrenness? As I sit here on the porch overlooking the place where the last two years of my life developed, I'm not sure if I'm dreaming or vividly awake. My mind sifts through the timestamps of the last 48 hours and I cannot seem to pinpoint the exact moment that everything changed. It's like that, change. It creeps up on you and before you know it, you're sitting in the aftermath of what's been *a long time coming.* The sun sets. I don't think I've moved in awhile, definitely feel like I haven't taken a breath in consecutive moments. Is this what dying feels like? Stillness. Lifeless while being alive. The little warmth the sun granted me now slowly disappears. It's dark now and I'm still in the same position I started in on the porch floor. The same porch we used to laugh on, and randomly, I caught a glimpse of an eerie happiness.

What was that?

In the middle of the most devastating time of my life, I sat on a cold empty porch, and smiled. It didn't feel like it came from me. In mere seconds I was overtaken by something else…

but what?

Who?

Then the coldness returned. A void, the kind of hollow emptiness that echoes for miles and miles. It's the kind of emptiness that doesn't seem to have an end. My eyes darted back and forth searching for an end to this cold pain inside me. At that moment I found myself wondering how this story would turn out. What's on the other side of my world being turned upside down?

I felt like pennies being dumped from a purse. Scattered. I wondered how you can start planning for the beginning of something, only to be met by a swift end you didn't see coming. I had begun to conceive in heart and mind well before the baby ever lived within me. And there I was in the very next moment, sitting at a funeral before the dream ever gave birth.

There are moments in life where you meet the end of a thing. There's no warning. There's nothing you can do to prepare for this moment, yet your whole life has prepared you to make it through. Sometimes a death is news to you, but the earth sings anthems of your victory. And though the road ahead seems treacherous, you'll pull through, but not without dying first.

Ready or not, here it comes.

PART 1

SUDDENLY

Sometimes the anxiety you're experiencing is because internally you know you can't stay *here* any longer...

CHAPTER 1

1 Day Before Day 0

It's 6:00 p.m.

I was getting ready for a public speaking event and just moments before the event began, Sam started a fight. Typical. At this point, I should have expected it. I sat there as he shouted about how I cared more about work than the relationship. Perhaps that was true. It wasn't in the beginning. My work was something I could lose myself in. Something I could trust. It was simple math to me. What you put into something is what you get out of it. With him, I had thrown in years of effort and the return on investment wasn't looking like a profit. I continued to let him yell, with no response. He stormed away just minutes before the event began. I wondered if this was normal. Isn't your partner supposed to be your peace before you go out into the world to do amazing, challenging things? Was support too much to ask for? Was I not worth being celebrated?

I took a deep breath and put on my game face. I had hundreds of people waiting on me to deliver. This wasn't the time to crumble. The most curious enigma is how one can smile while their heart is dying. This was just another one of his antics. He wanted me to affirm his place in my life and the reality was I had nothing left to affirm. He could feel me giving up before I ever uttered the words to myself.

I feel like an innocent bystander who gets caught in open fire because I was in the wrong place at the wrong time. I had my own internal work cut out for me, but I couldn't carry him too. That's me. Sometimes I play savior and end up dying in the process. Several wounds to the heart. This isn't a good reflection of what's ahead and now I'm questioning if I even want to take another step with him. Why take another step if I'm doomed to fall? Why take another breath only to be choked before my lungs fill with oxygen. Better not to breathe in at all, I suppose.

I smile. All eyes are on me. As I begin speaking, it occurs to me that no one watching would ever know the pain I carried in my heart that evening. I was convincing that way. The type of person who is on the verge of a mental breakdown and you'd never know it. I was good at masking my pain.

Until I wasn't…

I'm angry and I'm tired of these moments that break me.

I don't want to talk about me. I want to talk about him. I don't even know how to talk to You {God} about these experiences and emotions because I feel like You brought us together knowing full well I'd have to deal with this. You say You protect me but does my heart fall within that contract? Heartbreak is never fair or maybe it is my fault but regardless I'm left to pick up the pieces of my emotional state alone. I don't feel like You are in this with me. It just feels like You're watching to see what I'm going to do next. Forgive. Let go. Move forward. That's all I hear from You. *Do something.* Maybe it's not You, because You've taught me guilt doesn't come from You. Today feels like pressure.

Respond?

React?

Do something, but what?

When I talk to You, You tell me to focus on myself, but I don't see You deal with him. I always have to adapt to situations I never asked for. I don't want to continue my life like this. I'm Your daughter so why does my heart have to keep being broken by this man? Where are You at in this?

Or are You in it at all?

It's clear I don't trust him. I don't trust him to be able to make decisions on his own that are preventive. It's always in the aftermath that he learns. How can you be married to an adult yet feel like you're raising a child. It's hard to trust him to lead when I'm left to fix a bad decision. I'm tired.

Why am I still here?

What's the point of all of this work because I can't fix him and it doesn't feel like You are in this with us. Life feels similar to a bunch of attacks to the same wound. As soon as something begins to heal, another blow opens the thin threads that once connected the fragmented pieces. I lose trust while I lose my mind.

I don't want to waste time thinking about him anymore. I don't care what he does. I'm tired of putting my heart back together only to stand back up and with one blow it's back in a million pieces. Why bring him to me to break me? Or did You bring him at all? Did I choose this life failing to realize what I signed up for?

I've proven I can forgive. I've moved forward. I've let the pain go. But this is my life with him. Constant uncertainty. Two great weeks and one sucky week. Back and forth. No stabilization and less trust with each passing moment. And for what? To some degree, You are allowing this to happen, *right?* Rescue me from myself, from what I can't see. Show me the blindspots. I feel crazy and I can't remain in this space with him any longer. My life feels like a game. A joke. A waste of time. Is he a great person? Yes. But is he great for me? A question I already know the answer to.

A part of me wants an easier route. Sometimes I think if he was erased from the equation, I'd be a lot happier. No worries, no second-guessing myself. No insecurity. I miss the confidence I had in myself. How do you knowingly walk towards the death of a relationship realizing you're inevitably going to break into a million pieces? Some days I feel I have no choice. As if I'm being forced to walk in this direction, forced to shed the remnants of me.

Which one do I choose? What's known or the unknown? Give someone another chance or take the little dignity I have left and move on with my life? To fight or to wave the white flag? To be honest, both roads feel like a massive failure. Truthfully, the divorce feels inevitable. Suddenly, I wondered why such a difficult choice began to seem so easy. There are moments in life where you're given evidence. Circumstances come to reveal the reality you squint at with both eyes barely open. Most of us don't want to see what we truly see, yet this is what we asked for somewhere along the way. We asked for the truth. Then it comes in the most disgraceful way forcing us to meet a pivotal cross road. A choice must now be made. What do they say? Ignorance is bliss. In my case ignorance equals heartbreak and I'm not so sure I want to continue on in brokenness.

Maybe I'm better off alone. Maybe it's me. Maybe I'm just not cut out for relationships. Maybe I'm not meant to put my trust in another human...

I'm beginning to be disgusted by these cycles. At what point does one jump off the merry-go-round of disaster? Yesterday's fight didn't make any sense to me. I had just recently reached a new height in my career. I was helping change lives and providing a solid income for our home. And just when I thought we'd hit a new level of happiness, he'd throw some wrench in the equation and with it, kill all energy to celebrate my success. Interestingly enough, I saw it as our success, but he didn't see it that way. I was becoming public enemy number one in my own home. Some people are so afraid of your success because of how they let that success reflect on them. Some people will be there to cheer you on, or they'll be there to distract you from destiny and sabotage what's rightfully yours. You'll see the pattern when you reach a new height and those who were once with you turn and walk away. It's never really about you, and always about them.

All I could think about while I spoke to the audience was, *this marriage is a trap*. I'm suffocated by the idiocy of a man who learns through my pain. I knew I had a choice to make and it ended with me being alone. No matter how much I wanted to blame him, I too played a pivotal role in staying. One can only continue what you allow. It was no one's fault. I played the main character in my story. Sometimes the harshest reality is realizing the role you played in your own undoing.

The event ended. I sat in a dark room wishing he'd be there to congratulate me. Hoping he'd come through the door and scoop me up, whisk me away to dinner, and tell me we'd be alright. Why do we want love from the most painful places? I managed to grab my belongings and walked outside to catch an Uber. When he stormed off, he took our only car with him. It sucks to feel abandoned in multiple ways all at once. I should have felt exuberant. I had done a smashing job. I've always been good at what I do, but even the high of an accomplishment couldn't mask my bruised heart. I sat in the backseat of the car. Thankfully the driver kept his trap shut. I wasn't in the mood for small talk. Dazed. I checked my phone. I didn't have any messages from him. No missed calls. Just silence.

In the middle of the inevitable, there's this crescendo in life that I feel…

…like the bridge of a song where the key is about to change, but it hasn't yet. Life feels like it's announcing something I couldn't or wouldn't have expected. Anticipatory, that's what I feel. And although my heart wants to safe track my own destiny, something calls to me from beyond…beckoning me to run towards the glimmer of light. The speck of hope. *Run forward, go boldly.* But where?

Curious the way life feels as if it's running from me but not in a bad way...or maybe I'm running after it at a speed I'm not so familiar with. How do your legs adjust quickly to movement when you've been resting for a season? Internally I sense the next few pages of my life will require long distance running. There was no warming up for this place and I have a feeling this phenomenon is only going to continue.

I walked in the door of the home we'd spent the last two years in.

I didn't call his name. Part of me knew there would be no answer...

You can't give away what you don't have and you can't explain in part what you don't understand. Now is the time to sit and be a *student*.

CHAPTER 2

Day 0

———

Last night I came home to an empty house. No sign of him anywhere. Sam left.

He had done this before. The routine was to throw a tantrum so he could be reminded of my love for him when I asked him to come home. He never truly wanted to leave but this was the easiest way to get the response that made his heart feel safe. Tragic. This story was familiar. Earlier in our relationship he'd tell me that his mother did this to him and his siblings. She'd get angry, tell them to pack and leave and just before they'd leave, she'd run after them. If they stayed, this communicated to her that she was loved. I'd found myself in a generational cycle. In the deepest parts of my heart I felt sad for both her and Sam. What do you do when you want to help someone you love heal but it costs you in the long run?

What he didn't realize is that every tantrum he threw was another chip at my heart, and more expeditiously my patience. A couple solid weeks and a couple chaotic weeks. It was becoming very clear what the next few years held for me. In no way was I perfect. Of course I had my blindspots. But how many more times can someone threaten to leave before the other partner no longer cares if they're present or not. The threats become redundant and the fear of losing someone slowly fades away. What's left? You begin to see you're more than okay without them. In a sense, I was learning to live without him well before he'd ever gone.

Pack and leave. Pack and leave. This wasn't a new experience for me, only this time it was. We had just decided to expand our family. Rewind one week and I was on the phone with my family telling them we're trying to have a baby. I was already planning what the nursery would look like. Pinterest pins flooded my home page. It's uncanny how your life can change in a few moments with no warning that change is on the horizon.

He took the only car we had. Just 34 days ago I was hit by a drunk driver. My car was totaled. I'd never been in a car crash before. And to be honest, I shouldn't have survived this one, not without a couple missing limbs. The police reported the driver's alcohol limit was three times over the legal limit. It happened at night. I was hungry after leaving church. I craved a spicy chicken sandwich from Wendy's. Seconds after I pulled away from the drive through, a large yellow Hummer came down a hill at full speed and crashed into the middle of my vehicle just inches away from the driver's seat. He hit me so hard, he pushed my car out of the way and kept rolling down a hill only to find himself stopped by a dense pole. The vehicle parted like the red sea around the pole. I'll never eat a spicy chicken sandwich from Wendy's again. Too many memories. Once my car was deemed totaled, we bought a beater together just to get us into the next phase of life. He took the beater so I was left car-less. I looked outside to see the beater nowhere in sight and part of me was relieved. It reminded me of that horrid night. I'd go on to spend the night in the hospital and relive the experience in physical therapy for months on end.

He sent a message saying he was done. This isn't what I wanted. If it was up to me, I'd stay and try again. Something within me started to feel like it was no longer up to me. As much as it pains me to think of life without him, I don't know if I can continue on in this way...If I took him back, who's to say after being eight months pregnant, he wouldn't pull this stunt again? I can't possibly welcome a baby into the world cradled in such uncertainty. Somehow in this tornado of a moment, I sit calmly on the bare floor lost in thought. I'm not sure how much time has passed since I stood up. In my anger, I moved all of the money in our shared accounts to the ones solely in my name. That would teach him. Grief can turn you into someone unrecognizable. I set a budget for the week and walked to the market to get some groceries for a couple of days. I think I'm going to buy a motor scooter or a bike until something settles with getting a car. I didn't even care that the car was gone. We spend so much money on things. When life hits, you begin to realize what's truly important and what can wait.

My walk is lonely. It's in this moment, the ones where you can't escape your thoughts, that I realize I hate him. I can't think about that right now. It takes all I have left not to sink into a dark abyss. I don't have the capacity to think about what hasn't happened yet. I'm still reeling from what has. In a few weeks, I'm going to my sister Delilah's. I have to be alone for a while. That trip seems lightyears away. I dread what might happen over the course of seven days, let alone a few weeks. It's hard to plan for a new week when one day changes everything in your life. Soon I'll be with my family. Something should break by then. God will speak to me about what to do next.

I called my mom as soon as I walked in the door. She would know what to say in the meantime. We laughed and cried in the middle of pain. This is probably the lowest I've ever felt. To walk towards ultimate vulnerability then feel betrayed is nothing I ever want anyone to face. It's a deep wound that can only be mended with time, attention, and pure love.

CHAPTER 3

Day 6

Every morning waking up has felt like a dream or maybe a nightmare. I wake up wondering what really happened and what was dreamt. Some days I hope my reality was just a dream, but when I roll over the empty spot next to me confirms what I hoped wasn't true. If you've ever met the day with grief, you know it's enough to make your legs incapable of holding you up just to use the bathroom. Opening your eyes and seeing sunlight feels like a job. I didn't ask for any of this and then I felt shame for wanting someone that chose to leave. My body felt split in two. Half of me felt like a victim and the other half felt like a warrior fighting me forward. Torn between missing what was and knowing there's more wholesome life to experience on the other side.

I spoke with my family on the phone today. This is what I noticed. Everyone was cheering me forward. Their words rang in my ears.

"Good riddance to him."

"He doesn't deserve you."

"You're going to find someone who really loves you."

"I'm glad he's gone because you deserve more."

It's like no one could see my pain. I'm not even sure if anyone asked if I was okay. Sometimes no matter how good the decision is to move forward, you need people surrounding you that can sit with you in the pain from today. Sometimes they see the future you before you've embarked on your journey and the you in the future is happy and whole, but today you really needed someone to just sit with you in the heartache and tell you it's okay to be sad.

My mouth was dry. Usually that happens when you've been talking for awhile but I'd only said a few sentences. There wasn't much to say. It was difficult to communicate the sequence of events that led to this place. I found myself holding the phone to my ear while their voices trailed off in the distance. The only thing that brought me back to life was how hot my phone felt against my face. I must have been on the phone for a while. I'd lost track of time. Eventually, I found a way to hang up. I just wanted to sleep. I think it has been over 48 hours since I last ate. Not even food excited me.

Still no message since his last text. No phone calls. More silence.

Information becomes revelation and revelation requires *transition* in order to result in transformation.

CHAPTER 4

Day 17

———

I woke myself up to a fully limp arm. My body weight crushing my right arm that lies lifeless underneath me. Trying to distract myself with something on my phone, I reached over to grab it but to my dismay, it was dead. I think often about how little I've written over the last few days. I'm a writer by nature. It's a passion of mine, but my thoughts run rampant in my mind. Everything is scrambled. There's no way I could formulate a grammatically correct sentence right now. So much is happening and not happening at the same time. I feel like I'm left to move in new directions, uncharted territory, because of other people's choices. What do you do when someone's choice completely redirects your life? Then I ask myself, what role did I play in all of this? Perhaps it was my choices that led me to this monstrous pivot.

My best friend Jesse came over tonight. I'd been pushing off spending time with her because I knew we'd talk about the recent events. I don't think I'd brushed my teeth at all today, and I had no plans on it. It was one of those days where you'd rather be indoors because you look deranged. I was fine with my disheveled hair and lingering morning breath. She came over in the evening and left at 1:30 am. I didn't realize how much I needed to be around people. It was nice to hear about the difficulties in her business, raising children, and what she had for lunch that day. She reminded me that people are still living in the world and I needed a break from the decay in my mind. She cooked me dinner, one of my love languages. I consumed it all so quickly I'm not sure I remember what was on the plate. I hadn't made myself something to eat in a while. We laughed about a comedic disagreement between her and her husband. I don't remember the last time I laughed. Shortly before she left, we installed a security system on the door. Sam was the type to pop up unannounced and I wanted to feel safe. We talked about everything and nothing all at the same time. It was nice to have a conversation that wasn't about me. I was able to get lost in her, like a classic novel. She opened my eyes to something…I was able to find rest in the life of another person. Call it a distraction, but it's exactly what I needed.

She gave me rest.

CHAPTER 5

Day 36

I'm packing for the family trip to North Carolina. My family is a crazy bunch of misfits and I couldn't love us more. He was supposed to go on this trip with me. Still no word from him. I look at my empty suitcase trying to figure out what to put inside. My brain cells feel like they're functioning at minimum speed. Actually, whatever capacity is below minimum speed is where I'm sitting. I think being with family will help. Simultaneously, I'm dreading being the only member there who doesn't have a significant other. Everyone else is married. Happily? Not my business. I was an outsider.

I'm exhausted. Tired of doing everything alone. Exhausted from all the errands. I went from a two income home to a single income home with all the same bills. I was left with all the responsibilities. Life changed overnight and I'm still catching up. I don't know how long the catching up will take. I feel like I'm running on a treadmill in the gym. Exhausting myself and getting nowhere. Running in place. I possess the coherence of a zombie. It's then that I realize I'm experiencing decision fatigue. I've still been staring at this empty suitcase. The last three weeks have been about making decisions. I yield. I'm just going to rest.

Wait, no. I can't just yet.

I hadn't cleaned the house since he left. Part of me felt like if I left the house in the same condition, he might return and it would be like nothing ever happened. Waves of mourning leave you gasping for air between guilt and shame. You wonder how you could want something so hurtful, but it's in your purity that you love deeply. I grabbed all the cleaning supplies I could muster and found myself standing over the bathroom toilet. Missing him turned into anger. I lifted the toilet seat to find his urine staining the porcelain. I growled while a tear fell from the corner of my eye. It fell fast as if it had been building up for some time. We used separate showers before. As if the urine wasn't enough, I scrubbed the shower with his pubes and facial hair everywhere. It was dehumanizing. To find yourself in pieces on the floor cleaning the remains of the one who didn't remain is…well, traumatizing. But I refuse to come back from this trip with more traces of him. He's gone. Like a ghost.

I've got to get out of this house.

I never took a pregnancy test. I didn't want to know if I'm carrying his child. It wasn't until halfway through the trip that I started my period. I was in fact, not pregnant. I'm not sure what hurt more. Letting the dream die as I felt my cycle begin or the fact that he never called to ask. Days were on the horizon where I would thank God for this blessing, but today…

Today I cried.

Note to Self: Sometimes the anxiety you're experiencing is because internally you know you can't stay *here* any longer…

If there aren't any problems to solve in life, create and enjoy the *absence* of problem-solving.

CHAPTER 6

Day 41

I woke up to cold sweats. In my dream I was surrounded by loved ones. People I didn't know yet and people who had journeyed with me created a circle around me. A woman in my dream told me I was going to be more than okay. She hugged me and walked with me through new doors. As each door opened, more love and more people surrounded me. Each door presented new faces, new love. Everyone called my name as if to urge me forward. I searched the crowd for the one person I'd hoped to be coming with me. He was nowhere to be found. No trace of his face as I walked forward.

I remember the dream vividly. If I saw each person's face today, I would recognize them. I couldn't fall back to sleep so instead I went to the living room, turned on the TV, and watched *The Notebook*. I just wanted to feel what I felt in my dream. Innocent love.

It was time to take action on the decision I knew lurked over me like a shadow. I opened my laptop while the movie played in the background and went to my email. I typed "divorce" in the search bar. Quicker than I would have liked the dreaded email popped up. I had reached out to a recommended attorney. She sent over everything I needed to fill out. For some reason I hadn't yet. There are moments in life that find you where you see something, or maybe feel something perhaps, and it gives you the courage to take the next step. Not the next ten, just the next one. For me, the next step was filling out the divorce paperwork.

I never thought I'd be filling out divorce paperwork. I mean, who marries with this end in mind. He was my forever after, until he wasn't.

Note to self: There is no *"should"* in grieving. Just after a death the emotions are at the surface.

All mixed up.

At times, you cannot tell joy from sorrow. There is no *"should,"* just grief. I don't have to feel I should feel a certain way.

CHAPTER 7

Day 42

It's two days before Christmas. I woke up this morning, had my green drink, then went on the patio to stretch in the sun. One of the beauties of Florida living is that you can stretch on the patio in December with barely any clothes on while people up north are shoveling snow out of their driveways. Feeling the sun on my skin reminds me of how alive I am. I've missed this, and by this, I mean feeling alive. Warmth and reassurance all in one moment. This has to become part of my routine in the mornings. I looked to the left and saw green hills. The clouds barely moved, as if to stop and admire the rich color of the field. For a split second, I had this feeling that I was going to be uprooted and moving to a new location soon. I haven't put much effort into moving. I begin stretching. What hit me about this moment is that it felt familiar. As if it's already happened and I'm just living out the reality of it.

Moments like this find me often. I'm minding my own business and a thought takes me drifting off somewhere as if my future self whispers a secret to me from beyond. She gives me hope. She tells me often, I'll be more than okay. That I'm going to make it, and not just make it but I'm going to be well. Then I realize what's happening here. It's one of those "Jesus winks." It feels so real, like I could reach out and touch what I see in that moment. It's Him giving me a glimpse of my future. Sometimes that's all you need to carry on.

JUST BEFORE DAYBREAK

Is the *memory* of a moment defining and directing my life?

CHAPTER 8

Day 44

It's Christmas day and I'm alone. It was somewhat of a choice and somewhat of a happening. My family invited me but I didn't want to celebrate. What was worth celebrating? My husband recently left so why would I go sit around a table full of couples only to be reminded of my pain? I frustrate myself when I don't allow myself to move on and be happy, but sometimes you'd rather be alone than fake happiness and that's okay. I did something I knew I shouldn't have done. Curiosity will either make you take a glance back or guide you forward. I went to Sam's Facebook and looked at his profile. I knew better than to do this. What I saw wrecked me. I knew better than to check. I knew whatever I'd find would be upsetting. And I still did it. It was a photo of him and his family from today. He was smiling. How could he smile at a time like this? This is the same family that he hated being around so who knows if this smile was genuine. This was me wishing he wasn't truly happy.

I'm angry that he gets to be with family on Christmas Day and I'm alone. It was my choice, but I should have been with him, not alone. His caption is really what set me over the edge. It said that he has a lot of time left in his life to live and although this is true, it felt like my pain was so easily brushed under the carpet. He doesn't get to get off that easy. He completely changed my life and...I hate this pain that comes out of me.

I hate it.

I shouldn't have to feel like this. I'm not the one who left, but I'm alone? I guess I could have spent time with my family but aren't we both supposed to be grieving? Social media isn't real. Emotions can draw a scary picture. I took an edible earlier in the afternoon and it's definitely settling in. Would this even bother me if I was sober? I don't want to feel this way about him or myself. I've got to start watching what I go to for relief. In my shame, I wish I never took the edible. In my freedom, I'm compassionate with myself because sometimes you just don't want to hurt. I made the mistake of trying to numb the pain while doing something that was impossible to avoid pain. An impossible setback.

Merry Christmas party of one. Instead of wallowing in self pity, I sobered up and went to see a movie. I thought maybe getting out of the house would help get me out of my misery but it only made it worse. All I saw were families celebrating. Joyful. I'm envious. If I'm hurting no one gets to be happy. How dare they? Truly, I was happy for them, sad for me. I grabbed some snacks and found my seat. I looked around and spotted couple after couple. Some holding hands. Some kissing. Some laughing. It's an ugly experience to feel hate towards innocent people growing inside you. Pain will do this.

"You have no idea what's around the corner" –that was a line from one of the trailers and it hit me deep in the chest. It felt like the last tug of hope I had in me to expect something amazing from my future, but then it reminded me that what happened to me wasn't expected either. I found myself reeling in fear of what else I might have to go through. I'm quite exhausted from having these intense moments that speak to this grand future, while living in the drudge of the present.

I left the movie early…doing things alone just isn't fun. As I was leaving, a party was going on outside the theater. Just made me miss Sam even more. One of the most confusing things in life is to miss what brings pain. I know in my heart I have to move forward, I have to end these dysfunctional cycles. It hurts because if he asked to see me now I don't know that I'd say no. Right now I just miss the comfort of being with my person. I miss being held. I want to hold hands during a movie. I want to kiss, to be intimate, to laugh and love. To be silly. I miss having my person. I'm standing outside of a sushi bar now waiting on food. Some days it's really hard to see the other side of this.

I walked in the door, collapsed on the couch and started praying. It was one of those prayers where you really don't know what to say…

Instead of keeping those wordless feelings inside, I decided to speak.

"I don't know what I need to do at this time of my life. Sometimes it feels like the weight of this relationship with You {God} rests on my ability to perceive what You're doing in my life and follow that but most times I get it wrong. So You can imagine from my perspective it feels like our relationship is failing. Or at least I'm failing and to what degree, I'm not even sure.

I don't know whether I need to fast. To pray more. To leave it in Your hands. To wait on You, to charge forward, to stay still. To observe or to respond. I simply don't know. Internally I believe you can do anything. You possess the ability to blow my mind but then externally I'm met with a reality that feels more real than You sometimes. It's only because I can see it, touch it, experience it. Not because it is more real.

I've never been HERE before. There's no rulebook for this part of my life. I'm doing the best I can but even that feels like it's not enough or like I'm walking one way and You're walking another. There's a distance I feel between us and I feel like it's because of me. Life feels like I'm running down a dark hallway with a bunch of doors unsure of which one to open and which one to keep closed. I don't want another door that creates more distance. This is the cry of my heart. How can You be within reach, within my next breath, but feel so far away? It feels as if You could yell and I would only hear an echo because of this distance.

Half of me believes this and the other half knows You're within me. What do I do, Lord, when I'm hanging on for dear life and only Your next word will sustain me, but it doesn't come? You will rescue me with Your mighty hand. You will show me where to go and what to do next. I trust in Your goodness. I've seen it happen before. If not in my life, then in the lives of others. I've read stories about how You showed up. I've sung songs about Your perfect timing.

There's no way You'll choose not to give me life and withhold Your good words from me. You will lead me. You are My Good Shepherd.

I don't remember falling asleep.

I never ate my sushi.

An *inevitable transition* within you is like a fetus in the womb. Once it's been conceived there is nothing anyone can do to speed it up or prevent its arrival.

CHAPTER 9

Day 45

I noticed the sun didn't hurt my eyes when I woke up this morning. I practice my morning stretching routine on the porch overlooking green hills. Something about those perfectly manicured hills allowed me to sigh. In a moment, I felt seen. I felt relieved. It was on this day that I forwarded divorce papers to his email.

My days still feel stale, but I've gone to the gym a few times to work out. A couple of times, I went, sat in the parking lot, and drove straight to Krispy Kreme. I would get home and eat a dozen hot glazed donuts in record time then watch a comedy, never laugh, and fall asleep. When I woke up from my nap, I saw his name on my phone. My heart froze. It was a text and part of me didn't want to open it. It's been 45 days of radio silence. I think I stopped breathing.

NOW?!

What could he possibly have to say? My stomach turned in knots. The text read:

"Can we postpone the divorce?"

How does one have all the confidence in the world to move forward and a text message turns you into a puddle of water. My blood boiled. I raged inside and out. I screamed in a pillow and cried on the floor. I walked around the living room yelling at him as if he was there receiving every emotion I'd felt for the last 45 days. How dare he? How dare he ask for another chance? It's been 45 days with no word and the first response is to postpone the divorce? Not *"Are you okay? I miss you. Can we talk?"*

I stood there after pacing for exactly 17 minutes. I realized just now, I hadn't reached out to him either. How could I be mad that he didn't fight for me when I had stopped fighting too? For the next four hours I would read the text over and over and over. Getting mad all over again. I stood up and yelled, then cried, then sat in silence. Rinse and repeat for at least 20 cycles. This was a new level of crazy I'd never experienced.

I didn't respond.

I decided to muster up a little courage and go to church that night. It didn't feel safe to be alone with my thoughts regarding his text. Although, the entire drive there I wanted to turn around and drink myself into a coma. My pastor looked directly at me in the middle of service and in front of everyone said to me, "I can see God sewing your heart back together. I know it's heavy, it's a heavy mantle to carry, but that's because He can trust you with it. Keep going forward." I sat there with my mouth open. No one knew what happened just hours prior. Part of me felt like she was talking only to me. We locked eyes while she spoke. Her words felt like a release and as she ended her sentence, the flow of tears fell from my eyes faster than I could wipe them away. I sat in my chair and in my heart I told God "either way."

If He told me to go back to Sam and give my marriage another try, I would even if it crushed me. There are moments in life where God reveals your heart to you. You won't know what He sees until you speak certain words or pray certain prayers. These words don't come from memory, they come from experience. It was at this moment I realized I had broken an inner vow I made years ago. *I would never be the one who was abandoned and then give the one who left me another chance.* I was willing to try again. I would see this later as a strength in the middle of what felt like total weakness and vulnerability.

Wisdom involves an opening of blind eyes and sometimes that's more painful than remaining blind. It's an internal suffering that only someone who was blind can feel. A new exposure to sun, to heat that burns the retina of fresh eyes. Scales have fallen off and what *is* has become clear. Go boldly. This is what I felt in my heart while sitting in church. Boldly forward or boldly back to Sam? I sat around people praising God for His goodness while my world was spiraling. I sat there not being able to open my mouth and sing. I knew He was good but I didn't have the energy to hope. It took all I had just to walk through the doors and sit, let alone stay.

It's interesting how you can have such strong conviction and in the next second face indecision.

Home doesn't feel like home anymore. It feels like a cave or my grave. I knew I was dying.

I walked down the long hall and stopped by my office on the way to bed. A yellow sticky note pasted to the window caught my attention. I walked over and read it out loud. "What's coming in your life doesn't change what God has said concerning you. It also doesn't change what He has revealed to you already. There is nothing to fear."

That was written on November 2nd....Sam left November 11th.

I opened his text and responded.

"No."

When your mind is in a place of *desperation*, you'll take whatever you can get... when your mind is *well-rested*, you have options.

CHAPTER 10

Day 62

———

I can't sleep. There's so many voices in my head. This has got to be the most noisy my life has ever been. I experience many things all at once. There's no way to sort through them. I'm not even sure where to begin.

A billion things telling me I wasn't worth staying for.

I'm missing someone who no longer exists in my life.

Then I'm mad at myself for wanting tainted love.

I hear God say just hold tight. Wait. Trust Me.

Then I hear others say go for it, you got this!

I'm losing weight because I have no appetite.

Then I over-consume to the point of sickness.

I find myself getting excited about new work projects.

Then I'm depleted because I also have to completely redirect my life since it's just me now.

I think I need therapy.

It's frustrating because my hope speaks to the happiness I should have but I'm simultaneously so lost, I feel like I'm waiting for something to happen that's not going to happen. Just too many voices. I can't even hear Him {God}...

I've been trying to sleep since 8:30 p.m.

I'm recognizing that even a new opportunity won't mend my heart, it'll just distract from the healing I need. I need to be made whole and one moment with Him {God} will do it. That's not going to come from an email. A DM. A new work opportunity. More money. I have my dream car and I'm drowning in noise. I was finally able to purchase my dream car. A Ford Bronco. I learned many things while sitting in the dealership. Nothing material will ever heal open wounds. As exciting as it is to watch a dream become your reality, if your heart isn't healed, the happiness will be temporary. I wasn't looking for happiness anymore. I wanted joy. I wanted to be made whole on the inside.

I'm drowning in the unseen. Drowning in my thoughts.

CHAPTER 11

Day 98

Today I just feel over it. Over hope. Over trying. Over love. Over relationships. Over what my relationship with God looks like. Over opinions. Over my physical appearance. Over voices. Over recognition from strangers. Over being noticed. I'm over all of it. Numb. I think if someone stuck me with 100 needles I wouldn't feel a thing. Unfazed and dazed. Feels like I'm in a time ahead of myself and I could care less to "promote" myself in any way. By promoting myself, I mean performing any level of self care.

In moments like this, I try to find the truth. I know I love to write. Document. Reflect. If I could do that on an island for the rest of my life, I'd do it. Maybe I can do that now. Well, not the island part but the writing part. I feel empty and numb. Not really sad, just numb. I care about little these days. I'm not really sure where to go from here. I don't really want to teach or speak although it's part of my job. How can I possibly feed others when I'm starving? Freezing temperatures wouldn't faze me. Scorching temperatures couldn't burn me.

I decided to go on a trip with my sister. She's the epitome of joy wrapped in a Christmas bow. I knew we'd have a great time together. She's one of those people who can make you laugh so hard when you were just crying moments earlier. Sometimes you just need to get out of a familiar space and see something new. As I climb into her car, I'm already somewhat regretting this trip. I just want to be left alone. I want to crawl back into my grave. Indecision hits you at the most pivotal times. Curious...I have everything I've wanted in the last few weeks. A new Bronco, a new hair-do, new clothes, I even bought some new bedding to spruce up my bedroom, and yet...having it all doesn't feel like I thought it would. It's all a gray fog. I don't even know what I want anymore. I watch people drive past me in the passenger seat and I can't help but wonder what's going on in their lives. Are they happy? Are they sad? Do they feel loved? Do they yearn for more? Do they feel soulless? Is their heart hurting? Who is the last person they spoke to? Was it a good conversation? When's the last time they laughed? Do they feel peaceful? Are they really living?

Am I living?

Is this what it feels to be disconnected and unattached to things because it feels empty.

JUST BEFORE DAYBREAK

It's okay to be a *novice* while living between yesterday and tomorrow.

CHAPTER 12

Day 178

I stand looking in the mirror half laughing half crying.

My life is crazy. Some days I feel like I can't catch a break. Today I scheduled to have my micro links taken out. When I went to my hair appointment four months earlier, I didn't even know what micro links were. My stylist walked me through the process. I was ready for a change, sometimes that starts with your hair. Fast forward 4 months and I'm sitting in the chair watching clumps of my hair fall onto the floor. Turns out the way they were installed wasn't the best choice for my hair type. I should have done my research before committing. I learned not to be so desperate for change that you don't study a thing before adding it to your life. Big lesson, simple example.

Now I sit in this salon basically hairless.

I had a feeling this was coming. I just didn't know in what way it would materialize. More change. I can't help but feel the outward changes are symbolic of what's happening internally. I didn't wake up thinking today I'd lose ten to twelve inches of hair. My hair was so full, so beautiful before and now it hangs like straw around my shoulders. It's time to cut the dead ends, again. I've been here before. It happens every time there's a major transition in life, only the last two times I cut my hair, it was voluntary. This time it's a hair emergency, not some chic haircut I've been planning for.

I spent two hours calling around to every shop I could find and most of them were booked out for the next month or two. I sat on the bathroom floor and cried after calling my sister and laughing on the phone with her about how comedic this day has been. Only it wasn't really funny. I'm crumbling on the inside. It's funny how simple things like an eyelash appointment or having to cut off all your hair can send you over the edge. Just weeks prior, I left a lash appointment and cried the whole way home. The lash tech finished her work and handed me the mirror. It was nothing like I asked for and everything I desired it not to be. I didn't recognize myself and therein lies the root of the feelings that keep coming like waves.

I don't recognize myself.

This is what happens in transition. The simple things you rely on daily change all of a sudden and you realize how much of your identity was wrapped up in things that were bound to disappear inevitably. For me it was my hair, for others it's a strong body. For some it's their eyesight, and for others it's their memory. Transition is inevitable, and although I was having a catastrophic moment because of my hair, it was evidence of what was happening to me beneath the surface. It's scary to experience so much change all at once. I found myself eager to see what would replace the disappearing pieces. But when nothing did, I began to feel like grey matter. A question mark.

Who am I without _____?

In the spaces of transition, we cling to what's familiar, even hair. I'm trying to find ways to be kind to myself on this day. I woke up this morning and my mother called. If I could describe her, I'd say she's like the sun rising in the morning. Sometimes I believe the sun is eager to greet us, jealous of the time the moon spent watching us sleep. She's like that, eager to greet you. It's refreshing.

I told her about my hair situation and she said to me, "You know why this is happening to you right?" My sister sat next to her and I could hear her sigh that I knew for sure came with a hard eye roll. My mother has a habit of telling people exactly what they need to hear at the exact time they don't want to hear it. She means well. I shrugged and looked at her pointedly. She goes on to tell me this experience with my hair is symbolic of what's happening in my life, a *"ready or not change is here"* moment. I let her speak. There's no sense in interrupting her. Most times what she's saying is oddly accurate and timely. She went on to tell me that I've been here before, maybe just in another way and that there's nothing to fear.

All I wanted to do was hide the change, I didn't feel ready to wear my natural hair out. Maybe I wasn't truly ready to cut off the dead ends. This is why I scheduled the hair appointment. In an attempt to cover up the newness that I don't feel ready for, a question arises...

Am I in fact not ready or do I just believe I'm not ready?

Ten minutes later I decided to cut all my hair off.

Life feels out of control but it's somewhat because I feel like I couldn't have prepared for this on my best day, but I was prepared... just in *several ways* I didn't recognize until now.

CHAPTER 13

Day 202

Setbacks. We never see them coming until after the fact. I did something really stupid today that I'm quite ashamed of. Loneliness left unchecked in the mind will have you reaching for things you don't truly want. I went to therapy today and told my therapist what happened.

"I let Sam come over," I said with hesitation.

She proceeded to do her "say more" look without using any words.

It was around ten o'clock on a Saturday morning. I had nothing better to do that day but Saturday cleaning. My phone went off as a message came in. Sam. I noticed I wasn't nearly as rattled as I'd been before and smiled at my own progress. I opened the message.

Can we meet for a late lunch?

A part of me didn't feel like responding and the other half of me thought, there's no harm in lunch, right? I opened my contacts and went through the list of people I usually spend time with. This was part of my routine. In an attempt to appease my loneliness, I would spend time with a friend or my sister. This kind of therapy itched the scratch without the added side effects of responding to your ex and then experiencing regret.

For some reason, I responded.

Yes.

Immediately I felt sick inside, but I'd been through enough therapy sessions to check my own guilt. I thought, *I had overcome so much, there's no way a lunch would dismantle me.* We responded back and forth and before I knew it I was glossed up in a new outfit heading out the door. I knew better than this, but I pushed all of those thoughts out the window and hoped for the best. We met downtown. I wore my short skirt. The one I know breaks necks and makes you take a second look. I knew exactly what I was doing. I wanted to feel desired. It's been awhile since I'd seen him, so much that I wondered if he would look any different.

I checked my phone after applying another ridiculous amount of lip gloss to see another message.

I've already got a table, just walk in and then head to the left. I can't wait to see you.

My stomach dropped. I sat in the car. Why was I doing this again? This is when all the thoughts I pushed out of the window came back. I took a deep breath and put one foot out of the car. I came to and realized I must have been sitting like that for at least two minutes.

Look, you're here now. You're either doing this or you're not, but sitting here like a stunned deer isn't helping. I coached myself. I do this often.

I closed the car door. I was standing outside of the car. I guess I was doing this. As I walked toward the restaurant, I couldn't help but think all of my hard work to get to this point was about to be flushed down the toilet. Why would I put myself through so much pain to move forward, only to walk back? Flashbacks of sleeping on the floor and crying until

I couldn't see played like a movie in my mind. I could hear my heels tapping against the pavement.

I looked damn good.

I walked in and headed to the left like he said. There he was with a huge grin and my favorite drink on the table next to him. It was at that moment, I knew I should have run for the hills. My body seemed to walk involuntarily right back to the most pain I had ever experienced in my life. I slid in the booth and pinched my thigh on the way down. I needed to make sure this wasn't a dream. I had actively participated in making this moment happen and now I didn't see myself in any of it.

He leaned in and hugged me a little longer than I was comfortable with. I think he could tell I was uncomfortable. He was always great at helping me feel at home. He always made me feel like I could take off my shoes and relax for a while. That was the thing, it was only for a while, and shortly after, I'd find myself watching him pack his bags, or covering holes in the walls with decorative art from where he'd used his fists, or standing with tears on my face while being screamed at less than an inch away from my face. This was the exact opposite feeling of "kick your feet up and stay a while."

Now, I sat next to Sam watching him smile and admire my outfit. For a second, I thought, maybe he's changed. This was my hope. I drank the lovely ensemble in front of me so quickly, he asked if I'd like another. I indulged. I'm pretty sure it was so I could stop overthinking and deal with the consequences of the choice I made to be here. Time passed on and the sun started to set. We laughed and reminisced. He flirted and I obliged shyly. That was the thing about Sam and I, we weren't just lovers, we were best friends. It felt good. The kind of good you know is too good to be true. Dinner was fantastic. I'd always had a giant appetite, and I never let a date force me into eating a dainty salad at the expense of looking "cute."

He sat there staring at me. I looked back as if to say what. Before I could say anything. He leaned in and kissed me. I pulled away but it felt so good. The kiss seemed to wake me up. I sat there wide-eyed and in shock at this man, my husband. Isn't this what I wanted? I never wanted him to leave in the first place. This time, I leaned back in and placed an all-consuming kiss on his lips. His eyes still closed when I released him.

"Come over to my place? I'm not ready for this day to end yet," he coaxed.

DEANNA LOREA

Sometimes living in between yesterday and tomorrow feels like you've become *a vagabond.* Yesterday no longer feels like home and tomorrow's home appears vague and unfamiliar.

This was our dance. I'd seen this before. I guess this was one of those moments where I fell for everything because I didn't stand for anything. Sam was always so good with getting back in the door. As a matter of fact, he once bragged to my own mother that he would always be able to get me to take him back. My stomach turned at this thought, but I still shook my head yes.

He paid and walked me to my car. There was a buzz of excitement stirring within me. Perhaps I wanted something to happen. After all, he was my husband so even if we slept together it wasn't "wrong," right? We went back to his place and before the door closed, clothes were being ripped off. I knew what I came to dinner for and it wasn't to reconcile our marriage. He was the safest human to sleep with. I'd always been the girl who could never hook up with a random stranger. I needed to form a bond before giving myself away. He turned on music and dimmed the lights and sat me on the counter. It was over before it began. Pure indulgence. I enjoyed every minute of it. This was one of the things we were good at.

Sex.

We went on for what seemed like hours. Our breathing slowed down as the intimacy came to an end and I looked at the clock. For a moment, I allowed myself to be caught up in this dysfunctional fantasy with a man who I knew wasn't a part of my future. I indulged because truthfully I wanted to leave him with the memory of what it felt like to be with me. He knew it was good. It's a rare thing to find someone who will give their all to you. I love hard, so when I choose to love someone, I do it withholding nothing. If you've ever experienced a love so pure before, you know it's something to hold onto, even if you find it in a friend or family member.

I'm not sure how we made it from the counter to the couch, and then on the floor, but I found myself searching in the dark for my clothes. He opened his mouth and went on and on about everything he's lost since we were last together. Sleep. Sanity. Me. On this night I realized people will tell on themselves if you just let them talk. We all want to be heard. I began to hear desperation in his words. Regardless, I had already made up my mind. Maybe I was the heartless monster. I sat there and listened while he kissed my forehead and admired my silhouette in the dark.

This eerie feeling sank in. Nothing has changed. I could feel it in the pit of my stomach. Nothing has changed and nothing will change. This will be our dance if I go back to him. I didn't want to be swooned and sweet talked into a relationship this way. I'd always wanted safety and security. I'd always believed that my life, my marriage, would be a safe place of rest for me and my love. This was the exact opposite. Deep down I was always mentally preparing for him to leave. You can only cry wolf so many times before people start believing you, and I'd started living as a single woman, in heart, well before he'd ever left.

I brought myself back to this moment. The more I listened to him, the more I heard his convincing speech. It's like this speech had been rehearsed. He always knew what to say to get back in. Rich words with little follow-through, and I kept opening the door time and time again. He asked me to stay the night. I had nothing with me so I turned down his offer and made up some excuse as to why I had to get up early.

I've never been more disgusted with myself than at this moment. I knew what was going to happen the moment I said yes to his first text message. I felt powerful and disgusted all at the same time. I gathered my things. Something within me desired the upper hand and I didn't like that feeling. It came with remorse. He followed me outside to my car and asked when we could see each other again. I said I didn't know. I knew the real answer. He kissed me and I let him. For me it was a final goodbye, for him it was a hope for tomorrow.

I cried the entire way home. Shame makes you feel dirty. I was so confused in my mind. I rolled the windows all the way down trying to get the shame to somehow blow off of me and rid my mind of the gross thoughts that kept telling me how I'd just taken ten steps back. Sometimes after a wave of grief and loss, you just want to feel something, anything. For me, it was him. So I let myself feel only to realize nothing has changed. Perhaps staying numb a little longer would have been better?

If you've ever gone through a long transition only to make a decision and feel as if your progress was all in vain, you understand my pain. I was no different than someone who'd been sober for over a year and then had a wild night that cost them something. You begin to feel like all your progress. All the willpower it took to get here was just washed away with one choice. It's back to ground zero from here. It was day 202 and I crossed that out for a number 1. I felt weak, and even worse, messy.

I'd just finished my story and looked up at my therapist. I half expected her to look at me with disappointment. We'd done so much work together in this small cozy room. This was the room for healing, not setbacks, right? I'd paid so much money to be *"here"* in life and now, was it all wasted time?

She sat there with these eyes that I couldn't read. I looked to her to tell me it's okay but she never said it was. She never said it wasn't. Our session went on for another hour. We talked about how progress isn't linear and she asked if I was okay with my choices that night. She asked me how they made me feel and why. I realized the more I talked, the less ashamed I felt. It was as if two people were sitting talking about an objective situation that had nothing to do with labels or identity. There was no right or wrong in this room, just us talking.

She said one of the most profound things to me.

"Sometimes you need to take a few steps back in order to take more steps forward." I realized I wouldn't have seen that nothing changed with Sam unless I went to dinner. Sometimes closure is taking steps back so you can walk forward. She reminded me of the beauty of my humanity and the gift of feeling. I tend to lean on the side of perfectionism and am very critical of myself per my own expectations of how I think a situation should go.

I had all the clarity I needed. Up until our dinner, I struggled with inner conflict. Did I make the right decision? Did I quit on us? Should I have had more compassion? Was I supposed to help him heal himself? What part did I play in all of this? Where do I take responsibility and where do I leave responsibility with him?

I was moving forward with my life but my heart was experiencing ambiguous glitches. One of the worst things you can do is go forward without your mind being made up. Sooner or later you're bound to walk back. We all leave when we're truly ready. Some of us need more convincing, more evidence. That might mean more heartbreak or another sleepless night, but at some point we will have all the evidence we need and the walk forward won't come with one eye glancing back.

Sometimes you have to see a little more before you're fully convinced to move forward. It was that night that I knew in my heart where I was going in life, Sam could not go. It might be a long road ahead, but this was not the kind of life I wanted to live. I knew there was more and I intended to see every inch of it.

We wear progress like a badge of honor and setback like a badge of defeat. Neither is right or wrong. Progress and setbacks are like a compass guiding us through evidence along our journey. If I needed to know nothing was going to change through a setback, then it was actually progress in the end.

It's *okay* to be uncertain. It's okay to say I don't know.

CHAPTER 14

Day 231

Today I wrote a poem.

"Daybreak. Something has to break in order for the sun to rise. How much longer will I mourn for the night when morning is just on the horizon. It moves swiftly and comes whether I am ready or not. Something must break for the day to be positioned.

How much longer will you mourn for the stars that used to burn bright? What was, no longer is. How much longer will you mourn? Day is breaking and this sun will warm the coldest heart, these rays will give the hardest night new vision. How much longer will you mourn for what was?

Day is breaking. Fresh lilies are birthing. The bird sings a new song. How much longer will you mourn what God has passed over? This new thing is on the wings of daybreak. This new thing meets the first morning's opened eyes. How much longer will you mourn the days past, the places once visited, the titles you carried?

Day is breaking. Look into the tomb. He is no longer there. How much longer will you mourn the identity that hung on the cross with Him? Why do you mourn what is dead? What isn't anointed? Day is breaking.

You must get going. What you seek is in this new day. Follow forward. We must keep going. Follow forward. On these wings you won't mourn what was. Leave the old skins behind, day is breaking. Do not stay in the tomb. You will not find Him there.

How much longer will you mourn what is no longer blessed? Leave what was, just before daybreak. Follow forward. This is the new thing".

I haven't talked to him in almost a month. From our last conversation on the floor at his new place, I realized, I'll never be able to even be friends with him. I'm constantly explaining myself, being called passive aggressive, or having to prove something. It just won't work. We aren't compatible anymore. Much of the incompatibility stems from this concept: people who aren't healed don't mesh with people who are healing. There will always be conflict and that's okay. I'm learning you can't morph someone into something else so they fit into the new places you're going in life. You can wish for people to change all day but the reality is that they will change when they're ready. And if you're waiting for them to change, well, you only hinder your own evolution. I'd gotten to a point where my lack of growth was killing me, so I could no longer hold onto what was or try to carry someone into what's new.

You'll look back and see that during the moments you felt most stagnant, you experienced the most *growth*.

CHAPTER 15

Day 297

I decided to book a trip to Houston with my sister and our best friend, Ashley. Ashley is the kind of friend that always brightens any room. She's one of those friends who sings when she talks and has a thought about every thought. She'll be your biggest cheerleader and she's never envious of the beauty she witnesses in someone's life. She's a riot, to put it lightly, so I knew this trip would be nothing short of laughs and giggles. Between her and my younger sister, I knew laughter would be the essence of the next few days. I'm reminded today how important laughter is. With all the drama from change, and well, change itself, laughter can be the best medicine. In a world full of *adulting*, we must remember the freedom we receive while remaining childlike. Sometimes, in the middle of grief, the best thing you can do is watch a comedy or spend time with people who make you cry so hard you almost wet yourself. In the midst of laughter, grief and mourning seem to be less burdensome.

We landed.

I'm discovering much about myself on this trip. I feel like God is giving me space to see me. This is a gift. When He slows down time and gives you a chance to observe, He's giving you space to heal and truly *feel* without shame or guilt. I've noticed on this trip, I've been given precious moments that remind me of my humanity. I've been given time. Time to take a step away from the busyness of life and breathe. I'm an observer by nature. Lately, I watch my behaviors and observe what I feel uncomfortable in. I observe where I feel safe and well-rested. I observe when I feel scared or afraid. I observe when my body temperature rises and when I'm angry. I observe when I'm happy or experience joy. I observe deep sadness and grief. I've witnessed myself mourning, and truthfully, the moments of mourning have been the saddest experiences of my life. Loss can surface in many ways and come in many waves. I've watched myself weep on the floor grasping my chest trying to get in any little bits of oxygen. I've watched myself laugh so hard water shot out of my nose. I've watched myself sit on the beach and tell God all the deep secrets of my heart while the sun sets.

Sometimes you get to the end of yourself, where you can no longer not feel what you feel. There's nothing left to occupy your mind, no distraction to appease you for the moment. You're left with you.

Never take lightly the gift of introspection. It's in these passing moments that we really experience the beauty of our humanity. There is nothing shameful about any experience. I'm also learning in the past I've dwindled my own healing down to feeling an emotion and working through it. Although there's nothing wrong with that experience, I found myself trying to *fix* myself. Feel something, figure out where it came from and move on. In these new spaces of life, I'm learning to sit with the *why* of a feeling. I've never been told that can be enough. I ask myself why I feel a certain emotion and once I've answered, I leave it there. Intellectualization can be the enemy of healing. I've always wanted to fix anything that wasn't happiness, but when you can't fix mourning and there's no expiration date on grief, you learn to just sit with the feeling. It's good. It can feel painful, but this is the beauty of healing. I've been able to find rest when I don't try to move on from something so quickly. It seems to heal itself in time. Today it's okay to be sad. It's okay to mourn what was. It's okay to feel exuberant. It's okay to experience panic and anxiety. It's okay to feel like parts of you are dying.

It's in these moments where we really meet *us*. I've been able to meet myself on this trip and it's been more healing than I'd imagined.

After a long day of entertainment, my heart misses the quiet one can only find within. I snuggled up with a cozy sweater and went out for a cup of coffee alone. It's brisk outside. This kind of weather welcomes a warm fire and hot chocolate with a romantic movie. I decided to bring my journal along. One journaling technique I practice, specifically in public settings, is to find someone in my area and watch their behaviors. It sounds weird, but bear with me. There's a reason for this. I watch their behaviors and facial expressions. If they're with a loved one, I observe their interactions with their partner. I've seen people in pain. I've seen people in love. I've seen people who looked lonely. It helps me realize this: I'm not the only one in the world experiencing a tornado of emotions. There are many people in the world grieving. Many people are filled with sorrow. Many people are falling in love. Many people are escaping their realities just as I am by watching others live. The comforting thing

I find is that for just a moment, I'm able to take a step out of my bubble and glance at someone else's. There's a togetherness we all unconsciously share. While I journal, I notice I smile when other people smile. My heart feels heavy when I see someone who looks lonely. I experience joy when I see two people laughing.

We're much more connected than we think. Then I remember, while sitting alone at this coffee shop, I'm not alone.

There are really good things on the table for me. The past will tell me to find a reason why things are wrong when nothing is wrong *here*.

CHAPTER 16

Day 314

Today, I called the school and registered for classes. I can't explain why I feel the need to get my masters but it's time. I think I can finish it in two years or less. I have a feeling this year is going to hold many "first moments" for me. It feels good to do something new, to move forward with something I'm excited about. After considering someone else in every choice you make for the last six years, it feels good to choose what I want. With every choice I make, I'm finding *new eras of me* and it feels good to choose something for me.

Sometimes you won't know you've made a good decision until a year later. There's only one way to find out...wait and see and while you wait, *live*.

CHAPTER 17

Day 372

It's almost Christmas time. The holiday season tends to be the most difficult just after your life has changed dramatically. I want to be around everyone and no one all at the same time. Today is one of those hard days. I'm battling so much internally and it's safe to say most days I feel crazy. Sam messaged me two days ago. "Are you home?" That was it. I didn't respond because I don't know what that would lead to and I can't control a narrative that is uncontrollable. At this present time, I only feel angry because something was taken from me. The life I thought I wanted no longer exists. I'm not 100% sure the relationship was removed from my life intentionally but all signs are pointing to the intentionality being the answer. I've been more "me" lately. Even my family notices.

People are beginning to tell me I'm glowing. My smile is brighter. What used to hurt, hurts a little less with each passing day. Life feels like it might be safe to go outside and play for a while.

It's that feeling you get when you know something greater than you is at work in your life, but there's little evidence. You believe your pain isn't pointless but there's no glimmer of hope that speaks to it all working out in your best interest. You're somewhat existing within the grey area as grey matter.

I wasn't ready. I've been ready for very little that's happened this past year. The car wreck. The marriage ending. I wasn't ready for any of it, yet it all seemed ready for me. As if it was awaiting my arrival. Nothing rushed and in its perfect timing. Perfect doesn't always mean pretty. An interesting concept. He {God} remains the only constant in all situations as each occurrence has come and gone.

Healing feels like it's still lingering. Some days I feel like healing chooses how slow or how fast it wants to go and I'm left trying to keep up the pace. Regardless, He {God} and I are the only ones still standing. Everything else has faded away. Every identity I held so tightly. Every dream I planned for myself. It's all become a distant memory.

I'm not sure what's to come on the other side of December. My hope is pure joy and laughter. I've been through it this year in some of the most amazing ways, but a break from the grief and pain would be my request to Santa. My brain tells me I deserve a break from the pressing and crushing, but who am I to know when a break is truly needed.

In the last week, I've reached for things that used to satisfy me in the past. I needed relief. I felt disappointed in myself afterwards and so to numb the pain of feeling disgusted with myself, I took an edible as well. Sometimes you'd be surprised what you reach for during extreme states of grief. What happens when you're doing everything right and still things are taken from you? Then, because of the void, you begin to reach for things you haven't touched in years. It was in this week that I experienced a new level of the grace of God. I thought I was above the vices in my past and He showed me I wasn't, yet still, His love came down where I was and scooped me back up to Him. It was dehumanizing in the best way.

These are some of the choices I have to make in the next four weeks. Reach out to an attorney. Sell everything I have and start looking for a new place. Decide which classes to sign up for in the upcoming semester. Quit my job. I tend to be an extremist. I'm an all-or-nothing kind of girl. I might stay in the bubble of indecision for a few weeks, but once my mind is made up, there's no changing it. Full steam ahead. Every decision feels so large and so painfully irrelevant at the same time. Sometimes when we feel hopeless in one area, we try to overcompensate in other areas. Perhaps it's the lack of control in one area that makes the other areas seem so crucial, but truthfully, they aren't. Simultaneously I feel like I just need to spend every waking moment reading the Bible. I'm not even sure why. Spending my time on anything else seems subpar.

CHAPTER 18

Day 376

I came to dinner by myself at Bonefish grill. It was really nice. It feels like I'm celebrating a new page turning. It's been a whole year and I'm just now celebrating life. This moment wasn't planned but I think it's time. I no longer want to count the days since my life changed forever. I want a fresh start. I sat at dinner and smiled, reminiscing on the most painful moments of my life. If someone would have told me it would take me a year to think back to those moments and smile, I would have laughed. I don't always smile when I think about the endless lonely nights, but I am becoming grateful for my bravery to end cycles that weren't good for me, and with those thoughts come a smile. No one has come to take Sam's place and some days I wonder where my future love is, how

I'll run into him, and if I'll know he's my love just by looking at him? But I'm patient.

For a split second I catch myself off guard. The old me would never consider marriage again, never trust anyone, never want to feel abandoned, never want to be vulnerable again. Yet, here I sit, just a year after devastation, and I dream of what could be. Something in me has remained soft through such a hardening time. Sam's departure should have made me want to swear off men. But then I realize how much love in my heart I have to give and there's no way what's in me ends with him. There must be more to give, more to experience. In time.

I finally ended chiropractic treatment from my car crash, now the settlement from the car crash can proceed and Sam has filled out the affidavit so we can now move forward with the notary. This is the last step and I'm hoping we can schedule it before the end of this year. They said they would contact me in the next three business days with an update. Divorce can be odd. It can feel like departure and arrival at the same time. I don't want to go into a new year sharing his last name. Sometimes in order to be done with something, a quick clean cut must be made. No strings attached. Thankfully we didn't have any shared assets or children so the process has been fairly swift. At this moment, I am grateful that God didn't answer many of my prayers. Sometimes He {God} won't grant your desires because He knows what's coming and granting that request could make things harder on you than you'd imagine. I sit here and reflect on how life would be raising a baby without a father, without a partner. The thought makes my stomach turn. I sigh with relief. How is it possible that the things I cried and prayed for, are now the things I'm grateful I didn't receive?

An enigma.

PART 2

FINALLY

JUST BEFORE DAYBREAK

What do you do when what you *know* no longer feels like what you *know?*

CHAPTER 19

Day 1

I no longer want to count the days since Sam left.

Today begins a new chapter.

Today is my "Day One".

When life feels like nothing is happening, much has already transpired and is currently in motion. Perhaps there is nothing to do here but to *receive*.

CHAPTER 20

Day 17

A Poem I wrote about Blossoming:

Don't ever let life make you think you're motionless.

Don't let a seemingly wasted tear make you think you're not watering another seed within you.

Don't forsake the moments when you look at the soil and from your perspective nothing is happening.

If we were to time lapse your life you'd see intense development.

Struggle.

Movement.

Bursting free.

A flower blooming…

…buds bursting open at the seams.

…breaking free to feel the sun on fresh petals.

New colors and evolution.

Dead leaves falling to the ground only for more seeds to be scattered. Your life is in constant motion. There are no dead ends. No stillness. You are opening up every day. You are a new experience and a breath of fresh air to the world around you. And when you don't like how you look as a bud, someone else admires your color and shape…

…the way your leaves form a heart and the spotted blemishes that were really intentionally painted by design. Don't let life make you feel like you've stopped growing. Even in the ugliest of situations your time lapse would surprise you…

…that something so beautiful could sprout from a little black and brown seed is masterful.

As you are a masterful work in progress.

A blossoming flower.

CHAPTER 21

Day 38

———

I witnessed a curious moment today at brunch. I had just finished my favorite breakfast, crab cake Benedict with piña colada French toast when I looked up and saw an older man gesturing to a younger woman that her shoes were not tied.

I continued to watch and realized this was his daughter. He slid out a chair from one of the nearby tables and waved his hand in the direction of where she would sit down. She hesitated and began to look around and smile abashedly. We caught eyes and I smiled with her as if to say it's okay. She lifts her leg and places her foot on the chair. Her father proceeds to lean over and tie her shoe, his grey hair revealing this was no easy task.

He finished one and pointed to the other. She continued to look around at the people in the restaurant. We caught eyes again and I smiled back at her. I so badly wanted her to receive such a simple kind gesture without additional thoughts. I just wanted her to be in the moment with him. He finished tying her shoes. She couldn't have been older than me. Her appearance was youthful, her gaze innocent and shy.

I wondered what she was thinking. Was she embarrassed that someone older wanted to do something for her? Was she feeling judged by others because of his age? Did she feel she was an inconvenience to those watching?

What kept her from simply receiving? I wondered if she realized the magnitude of that moment or was she more concerned with what people were going to think of her, which is truly just a reflection of how she sees herself.

I saw myself in her.

Life has taken such a slow beautiful turn and I'm not used to not having to fight, to survive. My best friend Jesse showed up at 11:00 p.m. one night just to bring me leftovers and I felt guilty while I ate. I couldn't receive such a sweet moment because I didn't feel worthy. I didn't have to fight in order to receive something, this was unfamiliar to me. I then tried to do something to make up for such a thoughtful moment. Jesse looked at me as if I was crazy and I felt silly because why did I need to justify my existence?

She brought me dinner because she thought of me. My existence in her life caused her to be moved to action. All I had to do was eat, but in my unrest my brain was sent on a mission to justify the kindness towards me. The art of receiving can be one of the most uncomfortable feelings in the world. Everything inside you will speak to why it shouldn't happen when none of those reasons matter. We disqualify ourselves in the middle of receiving and miss out on a blessing sent to us just because.

I'm learning I don't have to do something good, or fight, or work hard just to receive.

Dolce far niente, the sweetness of doing nothing. This phrase has everything to do with receiving.

Feels like this entire year has been all about receiving. Things I wasn't ready for found me. I didn't have to do anything to bring them to me. There's something intricate about going through survival then somehow being "found" in a field of roses. In this new place, it's not about survival. The way you're used to going through life isn't applicable here. As a matter of fact, you have to release the mindset of all you've survived for this new place. The old rules don't roll over in the field of roses. There's no enemy trying to fight you here.

All you have to do is sit in this field and receive its beauty. It was all created for your amazing and pure enjoyment. If you're not careful, you'll become your own enemy with old ways and past behaviors. They can't be "here." This new place is restful. Situations come disguised as an attack but its presence only validates the reality that you don't have to do anything here. The attacks sort themselves out without a lift of your finger. All you have to do is watch the pieces come together seamlessly.

You can't sit in this field of roses with a clenched fist. They must be open to tend to the flowers that have grown here just for you. Your hands must be open to receive. The most significant amount of work you'll have to do in this new place of life will be to fight the old you. She cannot be here. She will whisper how things seem too good to be true. The old you will have you second-guessing the purity of this field of roses. She'll have you putting on armor to survive when you're supposed to be sitting smelling the roses.

This new place is about resting and receiving.

JUST BEFORE DAYBREAK

Transition can be a scary place. You have no idea what's on the cusp of tomorrow and *hope* is the only substance keeping you alive. Sometimes you glance at transition with one eye closed and the other half open hoping you don't see what you fear: nothing is changing...

Remember, there is a season for *everything*.

CHAPTER 22

Day 72

It's 7:23 p.m. The most interesting thing happened just now. I've had anxiety all day thinking about being in this house, and by this house, I mean my home. These new feelings came ever so quickly. The place I've lived in for the last three years of my life all of a sudden feels too small. Every room I enter carries memories of what was and for the first time ever, I begin to feel suffocated by the memories that live here with me. I already know what's coming. I'm going to move. This was one of those life moments where your mind catches up to what your body already knows is true.

For some reason, I couldn't bear the thought of more change, but the suffocation I felt from these walls wasn't going to allow me to keep breathing much longer. What happens when home is now your place of torment? I felt as if I was being pushed out of my cocoon. I wasn't ready to go, but if I stayed would I die? And where would I go next? My heart started racing again. The thought of being here for another year sounds worse than venturing into the unknown. I'm stuck here. I can't think outside of this place so I have to go. Sometimes in order to see yourself outside of where you are, you have to get outside of where you are.

I began to think of the life I created here. Would I move down the street? Another city? Another state? Leave my friends and family? What about my therapist, could I stay with her or just do telehealth sessions? What about Saturday night Bible study? There's so much I'm learning there, it can't possibly be time to leave. What am I holding onto? Routine? It feels like something is drying up and I have to leave. Like I've hit some sort of ceiling. How do I have more peace moving out with no plan than I have staying in my own home?

Interesting.

I hate where I'm at in life. I don't know where I'm going. I don't know when I'll leave. And I don't know what's next after this. All I know is I can't stay here. Maybe that's enough. Maybe that's all I need to know for now. Sleep is the only place of peace lately. I just want to stay asleep.

That night I took photos of all the furniture in my house. It was 2:06 a.m. when I finished cleaning and staging it all. As soon as I finished taking photos my heart stopped racing. I laid in bed and posted everything in my home on Facebook marketplace. I sat on the couch and grabbed the remote. *Avatar: The Way of Water* was a constant every night before bed for the last three months. Perhaps it's been the only real stability I've been able to rely on. I could get lost in another world. Relief, that's what it was for me.

I slept deeply and peacefully having no idea where I would be laying my head in the very near future.

This is what happens in transition. The simple things you rely on daily *change* all of a sudden and you realize how much of your identity was wrapped up in things that were bound to *inevitably disappear.*

CHAPTER 23

Day 96

I applied for my dream apartment: a studio overlooking the city of Orlando. There's so much to do surrounding the area, restaurants, shops, day life, night life, huge lakes for running, a new space to create a new life. After what seemed like holding my breath for consecutive months, submitting the application felt like an exhale. Things are changing for me. Slowly I am creating a new life.

In the very next moment I began feeling a little anxious because I'm trying my hardest to make something happen for myself. I'm trying my hardest to walk forward. For the first time in a long time I have hope for what could be…now…well, the expectation of a door closing is creeping in. When did I become this person that was afraid to hope for new things? I'd lived in disappointment for so long, I'd forgotten how to hope. Hope feels scary. Especially after heartbreak. Hoping reminds me of that feeling you get when the lights have been off for so long, you forget what daylight feels like. Light hurts your eyes until they adjust and you're able to see that the light didn't come to hurt you, but to reveal something to you. Perhaps submitting this application for a new home is my light in a dark place.

CHAPTER 24

Day 110

———

It's only 2:51 p.m. and I'm exhausted from the emotional drag and discoveries of the day. I pick up the keys in the morning. I'm eager to celebrate as tomorrow begins the next chapter of life, but I'm so tired from what it's taken just to get here. And so, my prayer is that whatever good comes my way, I would be able to enjoy it and celebrate it with full energy, not remain exhausted from having to climb uphill just to see what's waiting for me, then staying stagnant because I'm sighing in relief that relief came. I pray that He {God} will give me true rest. The kind that revitalizes and renews my mind so I am ready for whatever is on this next page of life. I desire the energy to truly celebrate goodness instead of being too tired from the climb to rejoice. I want to celebrate from a place of freedom and rest. The twinkle in my eye is the unseen smile, even if that dim twinkle came from a stream of flowing tears. I desire to smile with my face and with my life. If I am to be exhausted, may it be from dancing and laughter.

I've sold everything. It all had to go. There's something beautiful about traveling through life without being unattached to things. I've done this many times before, bought things and sold things. I wanted nothing more than to move into a new place and sleep on the floor if I had to until I was able to buy more furniture. The memories that rested in the fibers of the furniture couldn't come with me, and so I spent two weeks finding every piece a new home.

Work has been interesting lately. I get little opportunities here and there to make money but I do want something more consistent. For some reason I feel as though I'm just passing through many places in my life. I long for stability and consistency, yet I feel like a nomad wandering for a place that will be mine. It's been this way for as long as I can remember. Even with Sam, something within me felt I was just passing through. My relationship with God has been founded on rest. I don't feel any guilt or shame going through life. I don't always read my Bible or go to church or tithe. It's more than that and I wonder how much of that truly matters to Him? Maybe in another season it will be more important but not because of the act, because of what I'll receive through the act.

He {God} is giving in His nature. I've said this many times and now I'm seeing that He hasn't been preparing me for some "big call" I've been programmed to expect, and that only, but He has been molding me and purifying me so that when He brings good things, I don't self sabotage and feel unworthy. I simply receive. I'm learning with Him, this is the heartbeat of His intentions: for me to receive. He did this before I could ever do anything for Him and I sing songs about how He remains the same, so when did I change my view of Him and begin working for my worth? He hasn't changed…

Dad said to me earlier this year, just open your arms and receive. That God was walking me to a place of truly just receiving more than I could ever ask for. I see that happening already in small doses. A large dose would be overwhelming and I would push it away feeling unworthy of its weight. He's shown me the lost art of receiving through friends, through family, even strangers. Where people want to love me expecting nothing in return. It's been hard to receive and sometimes I had no other choice because of the place of life I was in. These are sacred resting grounds. He places us here so that we can receive all that is ours. I don't want to push anything away that He has already set aside just for me. I don't want human behaviors and learned cycles to dictate what I can and can't have.

Now, I can see myself. Good things are coming to me and I second guess their intentions. I become insecure and think *why me?*...failing to realize that I am God's daughter, an entire princess that He has sculpted and molded in His image. Nothing earthly can give me that kind of inheritance or status so everything on earth then cannot add or take away from my status in Him. He has done the work to reveal my identity. I've done the work to receive His words. Now when those words become a reality I become hesitant to accept them. It's one thing to hear the voice of God and another thing to see what He has spoken come to you through people, places and things...they find you.

He brings it all to you.

Am I, in fact, *not ready* or do I just believe I'm not ready?

CHAPTER 25

Day 121

———

I sit in this new empty apartment and cry often. Confused would be the word for the day, really the week. I don't understand how you can want something so deeply, get it, and then feel so lost inside of it. I remember just weeks ago desperately wanting to leave my old home. Too many past memories continued to haunt me. Isn't this what I wanted? A new space to breathe? A fresh place to start over? As I sit here and cry, I couldn't help but wonder why I wanted to go "back home." I was dying there, right?

My mom said it's okay to feel this way. I'm not quite acclimated to the newness of life and I cry because I'm grieving my old life. That happens. You can celebrate new life and grieve your old life simultaneously. You can smile and cry at the same time. You can miss something and have hope all in the same second. I realized today, I am experiencing many emotions internally all at once. I can be grateful for what I have now, feel blessed for a new chapter of life, and grieve the life I'll never have with Sam all at once.

How is it possible that the things I cried and prayed for are now the things I'm *grateful* I didn't receive?

CHAPTER 26

Day 156

———

I don't want this month to be over. I'm somewhat stuck in the bliss of what is and something in me is afraid it's going to end. That's the fear of the last couple of years talking. Sometimes you can't enjoy happiness right now because you're waiting for another wave of terror to hit when nothing is really coming. I was so happy or so I thought and then I wasn't. Overnight. The storm of life happened overnight. I'm still learning to rest in what is. That's not an easy thing to do when half of you is resting and the other half is standing guard just in case life falls to hell again.

My best friend Mary called today. She's the kind of friend that can go for months without speaking and then you end up gabbing on the phone for six hours straight. We've known each other for over ten years. She's a rare friend. One who found me during my time in Japan. I talked through some recent events and she listened intently. I found myself problem solving situations that truthfully weren't problems. I couldn't help but wonder if I was allowing a memory in my past to define and direct my life? I had become well acquainted with problem solving. In fact, from my perspective the last two years had been nothing but equations and solutions from a sudden moment. I was constantly looking for variables to control so I wouldn't end up blindsided again. This was my scope of reference. The beauty of it all is there's nothing wrong with problem solving, but when there aren't any problems to solve, your brain will create problems just to appease an old nature.

She spoke boldly as if to see something I could not.

Everything and everyone in life is a teacher.

If there aren't any problems to solve in life, create and enjoy the absence of problem solving.

There are some lies you've believed that *must die* so you can live.

CHAPTER 27

Day 201

The world is moving at great speeds. And for the first time in my life I can feel it. The numbness is fading. Observing the speed of life makes you realize how little space you take up but also how impactful your little space can be. Rapid. That's what it feels like. I'm racing to keep up with where I'm currently at while the earth moves beneath my feet. That's the easiest way to explain it.

Sam called yesterday. He expressed his desire for me by telling me he had several dreams that I was seeing someone else. He began to rant on and on about how everything in his life was falling apart. I think he was looking for something to pique my curiosity but the only thing that was true was this was another attempt to get back in the door.

It's interesting how someone can try to give you the thing you desired most but now it just feels like crumbs. I always only wanted him. His antics don't move me like they used to. I was grateful for his phone call. It showed me how much I've grown and how my heart is truly mending itself back together.

To hear he was really going through it was sad but I felt a release of the need to take care of him anymore. I can no longer be his source of support or his crutch. I have to walk on my own. I've seen God free me from the need to help others to soothe my own validity. But I don't have to help anyone right now. I can be the one to receive. God has positioned me to be the receiver and not the giver in this stage of life, although it happens naturally, it's not my focus right now. And so when Sam came knocking I didn't answer the door to be the savior. I answered it and then closed the door. I'm not sure I've ever known what that feels like. Especially with Sam. To no longer need him to need me or to want to be needed by him is freedom. The old me would have entertained him for the sake of feeling needed or wanted, not because I truly wanted him anymore.

I'm being set free.

God has done the work for me and I've surrendered enough to let Him give me heart surgery. It's crazy how I'm just now seeing the fruit of my labor. I'm just now seeing the harvest from my tears. I'm just now seeing that my decisions were sound. And the crazy thing is...I'd do it all over again just to be here.

The peace, love, and joy I feel here is the greatest gift. I've been given a revelation of who God is through the most painful moment of my life. He removes so I can receive. He prunes so I can receive. He's quiet so I can receive. He's timely so I can receive. He takes gut punches from me so I can receive. He's fine with having His character questioned so I can receive. He gives and gives of Himself so I can receive.

Everything I've been through this year, the hell and all, was so I can catch a glimpse of Him. A revelation that would conceive a new belief in me about my Father. He will go through great lengths to reveal the truth of His character to me. I'm grateful for the pits of life that take me low enough to where the only option is to look up. This is when I see Him truly.

I see His love for me never waived based on my performance. His smile towards me never faltered based on my abilities and achievements. He never turned His eyes away from me when I didn't want to look at myself. His gaze has always been steady and ready to pour out more of Himself. He gives and I receive.

The place I wept is the place where He met with me.

JUST BEFORE DAYBREAK

Even if you don't know your direction, you will be sure to find something *beautiful* along the way.

CHAPTER 28

Day 261

I'm a little sad. My dreams last night seemed to have some kind of impact on my day but it didn't feel like the thoughts were mine. It felt like they were being whispered to me. Thoughts I didn't want to keep around. Regardless, they were present so I had to dismiss them or continue to consciously carry them.

I have a fear that I won't have a place to settle in and call home, and I worry about what will stay and what will go. Is there a point to clinging to something that's fleeting? I can't recognize the difference between me passing through situations in life and what will remain. What sticks with me as I go? When you thought you were settled and life throws you upside down overnight, you adapt…

…barely holding onto anything or anyone that comes your way just in case it decides to slip through your fingers one day. It's like carrying your things in a suitcase with you everywhere and never unpacking. Never really settling into something because one day you might have to pack your bags and begin a new journey. Better to never unpack than to be caught foolishly setting up camp where you won't be staying. That's the PTSD talking. It's what my therapist calls prolonged grief disorder.

This isn't the way I wanted to continue through life.

It's hard to be attached to anything with this mindset. The truth of the matter is that it will all truly pass away. I'm finding some comfort in that. Everything. Even me. In this physical body, even I will pass away. Somehow there's a sigh of relief that pulses through me. I think it's okay to settle in here. There's nothing on earth that will remain other than my relationship with God and even that is shifting. It grows, so by nature, it changes.

I spent some time today redefining what is *home* for me. Transitions will have you questioning what's really here to stay and what's simply here to teach me something. Perhaps the two are intertwined.

Occasionally you don't feel like you're growing but then when you happen to revisit something from the past, you see just how much you've changed. You see just how much you've outgrown the very thing that you couldn't live without.

Sometimes you won't know you've made a good decision until a year later, sometimes five years later. I find myself wanting immediate gratification, but the truth is sometimes you won't know if the choice you made was good until much later in life. The question you have to ask yourself is, are you okay with living in the ambiguity of that choice? Will you be courageous sticking to your guns while you continue forward with little to no certainty that life will be more beautiful on the other side?

Along the way you'll have moments that find you speaking to the fact that you weren't crazy and what you followed blindly in the past was the truth. You followed a hunch and it turned out to work in your favor. This was one of those moments for me.

I booked my rental car and messaged Shanelle about the meeting place. I was in need of some long overdue girl time. My friend Shanelle lives in a small town I grew up in about three hours north of my new place. I messaged her again on the details for our trip before I left my house and triple-checked my suitcase. I hate that haunted feeling when you know you've left something behind but have no idea what it is. The drive to Shanelle was peaceful. There's something euphoric about the open road, the wind blowing through your hair, and a good song that results in your throat being sore from just how much you screamed the lyrics. I'd always loved driving. The world seems so much bigger, and my problems smaller, on a road trip, like everything is going to be okay.

I was about 3 miles out when I reached town. Something eerie sat on the city limits, but that didn't stop me from continuing. I looked to my left and right as I caught a glimpse of restaurants and shops boarded up with closed signs hanging in the windows. I whispered, nothing has changed. And that wasn't really the truth, it was worse than I'd remembered. It had been fifteen years since I'd last visited. This place seemed to be in some kind of time machine where the world around it continues to grow but this town regressed. Memories flooded my mind. I drove past the roller skating rink where I used to sneak out of the house to meet my friends. It was closed down. I saw my favorite pasta spot with boards covering the windows. What happened here? The school I used to attend looked exactly the same as I left it all those years ago.

A fog set over the town hovering like a spell cast making it impossible for anything to grow here.

The further I drove, the more grateful I became from my choice to move away to a new state at nineteen. It was a daunting decision. I had no friends or family on the other side, just me and a U-Haul. I left. I remember that feeling of knowing I'd encounter something greater on the other side. I wasn't even sure what I would find but I knew I couldn't stay here. There was no hope for me here. No place to grow and spread my wings. The place I used to call home was too small for me. I had left the nest and seen the world. Japan's exquisite dining, Korea's vibrant festivals, the hills of California and Germany's winters. It was good that I left. There's no way I would have experienced this life if I chose to stay.

And then it hit me.

This was a moment set aside in time just for me.

It was the kind of moment that says "keep going forward."

It was the kind of moment that says "you've done this before."

It was the kind of moment I didn't know I needed.

I have evidence.

I've walked into the unknown before and I have *evidence* that it was a good decision.

JUST BEFORE DAYBREAK

Sometimes in order to see yourself outside of where you are, you have to *get outside* of where you are.

CHAPTER 29

Day 298

I just finished more of my to-do list. The last 3 months have been so intense. The life of an entrepreneur isn't for the faint hearted. I'm a little angry tonight. Studying psychology brings out something in me. I realized I really want my youth restored. Every man in my life has abandoned his post. My father. My husband. I was thinking about filing my taxes this evening and I got upset because the one person I could depend on to help me quit. Random moments like this hit me and remind me that I'm human and I'm still healing. My therapist told me I need to change the story I tell myself about what happened between Sam and I. All this time later and I still have moments where the adult me wants to avenge the child in me. The truth about how we ended is that I said no more. I wasn't abandoned. I chose to move forward.

I can't stop crying.

There are moments when my armor wants to come back out. My armor tells me not to trust anyone. That love is silly and to always keep my guard up. My armor whispers that it's not safe to rely on anyone and that I only truly have me. With every whisper, I build an invisible impenetrable wall, one brick at a time. If I'm not careful, I'll allow past experiences to harden my softness to life. What happened with Sam was one experience, it is not the sum of my story.

I want to remain soft and pure. To be feminine and youthful, playful and adventurous. I want that so bad. It's like Sam took something I worked so hard to get only to be left with egg on my face. The truth is, he abandoned his post and I said no more to continuous cycles that kept me in bondage to heavier bricks and taller walls.

The last time we talked he said "when we separated"…as if it was a mutual choice. Another slap to my femininity and another brick added to the wall of my masculinity. I think suggesting it was a "we" decision hurt my feelings. Sometimes people won't take care of fine china and that doesn't dismantle the value of that china. The fragility and value are still within the china even if it's in fragments. Am I any less rare and fragile because someone drops me? In pieces on the floor, am I any less fine? Whether broken or bent, scuffed or impacted, I am still fine china. Valuable before my Father. Maybe I wasn't meant for the hands I selected or didn't select by birth to hold me. Maybe they weren't capable of protecting such a valuable rarity. Those hands don't decrease my fragility and the beauty of my rarity. They cannot any longer. I will remain rare, valuable, pure, and fine before Father.

He deems me rare and valuable. He will protect me at all costs. I will not become hard and bitter for being dropped and left in pieces on the floor.

I will remain soft and fragile. Becoming hardened will only keep me from receiving all that's already mine.

Are you willing to trade *all you know* now for the unknown road ahead?

CHAPTER 30

Day 332

My Pastor Brianne sent me this text last night at 11:30 p.m.

"Hi honey, for days I've been meaning to text you. I'm so sorry somehow each day got away from me. But I heard a word in my heart the day after I saw you. Since then it has been resounding over and over so I knew I had to text you. And it's literally just a word, like one word lol BRAVE."

BRAVE?

Another moment that found me. I find it curious when your existence is placed in the heart of another. Something compels them to respond or reach out. This occurrence is always for good reason. This is the least brave I've ever felt in my life. Some days I feel more like a coward. I feel brave for going to therapy. I feel brave for saying no to more cycles of stagnancy and manipulation. I feel brave for going to school for my masters. But for some reason, I told my therapist yesterday that I feel there's only been two times in my life where something amazing happened and I didn't have to do something to make it happen. I don't fully believe that's true but sometimes you feel like without your blood, sweat, and tears, nothing great will find you. It's a miserable thought. This is part of the reason why I feel like I need to do something all the time. If I don't do it, then it won't happen. It's the overconsuming self-fulfilling prophecy. This way of thinking tricks you into believing it's you against the world, instead of all things working together for your good. I sat there on that plush blue couch where I'd spilled more of myself than I'd imagined and thought...

I'm not doing anything to sustain myself, yet it happens.

I breathe over and over again without doing anything to make it happen. It happens naturally. There are facets in my life that require my participation and then there are serendipitous facets that don't require my participation. I don't always *need* to do something to make something amazing happen and I don't have to feel like nothing is happening in my life if I'm not doing anything. There are things He {God} is sustaining right now that are undetectable to the human eye. I can't see my lungs working but the evidence of breath tells me He is sustaining me. Good things can find me without added suffering. All I have to do is receive them and welcome them home.

Today would have been our 9 year anniversary. I learned something from therapy today.

She asked what are you fighting for? I thought this question was odd because I didn't feel myself fighting.

I said significance.

Those words came out faster than I expected. This was one of those times that you speak without thinking and then have to think back over what was said. It both surprised and shocked me that this is what I've been fighting for.

I'm learning you only fight for significance when you don't feel significant.

Herein lies the problem.

DEANNA LOREA

To run forward stumbling, crying, and uncertain is bravery. This is *courage*.

CHAPTER 31

Day 365

It's been one whole year since I turned the page in my story. I stopped telling myself Sam left and began writing a new story. I ended a dysfunctional cycle and decided to move into the unknown. That is what happened. A compelling thought: is a memory from the past dictating the freedom I have in the present? What labels have I placed on myself that continue a story I no longer want to read? I no longer want to see myself as a victim, abandoned, or left. I don't want to live in fear believing I'll never know a love that can stay. I can choose another story, and the one I've written for myself is that I loved so ferociously that I forgot myself. This is the beauty you receive for the ashes when everything burns to the ground. When I remembered myself, I decided to keep remembering myself and that meant leaving behind destructive patterns. This is a beautiful story. One of triumph and fearlessness. This story is full of pain and new beginnings. It's engrossed with deep love, innocence, sadness, and victory. It came with long lonely walks and the kind of hope that can only be found within your next breath. I felt deeply and to feel deeply is a blessing because it means you're alive. I've truly lived. I've worked through ambiguity and decided to take another step into what felt like a dark abyss. I've conquered mountains and refused to stay in valleys. I've journeyed here and it's not been picturesque. Sometimes you believe the journey ahead is teeming with fields of roses, but you'll soon realize those roses come with thorns.

To run forward stumbling, crying, and uncertain is bravery. This is courage.

CHAPTER 32

Day 391

Exponential growth.

There's a lot of quiet here.

There's something about the sensitivity of the stillness. When nothing is happening, you can see that everything is happening. One subtle movement causes your ears to prick up like a cat sensing motion no one else sees. In this place you'd be able to hear a butterfly's wings a mile away. It can be daunting. He {God} tells me to rest and what I've noticed most is the increase of sensitivity.

To what?

Everything.

Nothing is as it truly seems, and yet everything feels supremely intentional. How can both narratives be true? Sensitivity. I prayed for this. Last month, my request was for God to increase my sensitivity to the Holy Spirit within me. I didn't recognize that meant everything in life would come to a screeching halt. I can see Him answering my request, while He places a request before me.

"Trust Me."

Trust that if I ask you to sit down, resources will be provided for. Trust that if I ask you to step away, what you think needs you is kept by Me. Trust that as you rest, motion continues in My hand. He grants our request and in return asks us to trust Him. Even this is giving. It is His nature. I'll be honest, in this place of very little distraction, my anxiety has been the highest. How can the place of rest also produce the place of anxiety?

When distractions dwindle, truth surfaces. This is why I'm anxious. Once you are exposed to the truth you cannot unsee a thing. The anxiety is welcomed, as a matter of fact, it can feel required. Over the last three years, I'd found myself stepping into uncharted territory. I've noticed this pattern in life. Many times when I truly rest with Him, life is chaotic. Then when I rest in life, my relationship with Him feels chaotic. Where does my confidence remain? Which atmosphere must be sacrificed at the expense of true rest and peace?

Of course, I already know the answer but living this acutely aware of what I now notice feels like jumping into an alternate reality. One where time, money, pedigree, dignity, and obligation seems to vanquish. *"There's no time wasted,"* I hear Him say. He is the only One who can clearly differentiate stillness and stagnation. With Him, in stillness, there is no stagnation. We could be taking monumental strides together and simultaneously I feel as though I'm wasting time. Forever rushing to get back into the pool of proving my existence.

Forever proving my existence…

Transition is the bridge we must cross over in our *discovery* for truth.

CHAPTER 33

Day 427

———

Today was restful. Some days I wake up and the notion to just be with God is ever present. This is truly His desire with us. The day seemed so still as if it would pass as quickly or slow down seamlessly depending on my desire. We went through this day as I wanted. I chose the slow route. I found myself realizing my gaze was pointed but without substance. The kind of stare that doesn't hold anything in its vision. You're not really looking at what you see.

It felt nice to experience the awe of the day.

I took myself on a solo date, did some writing, grabbed a donut, and drove along the coast near Manhattan Beach. I thought, I will have a home here some day. I watched the waves pass me and felt the air on my cheeks while I drove with the top off of my dark grey two-door Bronco. This day came to bless me, as everyone in the past, and as everyone in the future will. Many things are uncertain in this stage of life, but I've become well-acquainted with the ambiguities of life. They don't easily scare anymore. Everything doesn't have to mean something, and nothing can mean everything all at the same time.

Yesterday, I believe I experienced every human emotion possible. All within 24 hours. I was physically, emotionally, and mentally beat by the time I went to sleep, but so grateful to experience the blessing to observe myself feel many things at once.

There's this intentional pause on the day. A call to just be here. I'm not sure what needs to be discovered. There are mysteries just waiting for your attention all around you. Much of me has died while other parts are being reborn. I feel life and death simultaneously. There's a page turning and I can't quite put my finger on what areas of life the incoming will hit, perhaps all. I can sense some gift coming to me. Something is earnestly on its way to me and I don't know when or where it'll make its grand appearance. Life is like that. Every day brings a new gift.

If life never changed and I had to repeat the same days, would I be satisfied with how I've lived?

What more needs to be acquired to equate happiness?

Days like this remind me that nothing added to me will equal more bliss. It all starts and ends with me. I am the beauty of this day. That sounds vain, but it's the truth of the matter. The day was created to greet me. It's all here for me to simply enjoy.

How amazing for trees, flowers, and beaches to be created simply for the entertainment of your gaze. Sure, they are here to educate, but in their rarest, simplest form, they exist as a thing of beauty for us to absorb.

Lovely.

There's an unheard melody that greets me every morning. It feels like refreshing water on a hot day. It's equivalent to watching a butterfly find you. It's the stability of the sunrise every morning. It's the consistency of the clouds moving past you. It's the stillness of an oak tree remaining. This unsung melody reminds me of a flower dancing in the breeze.

It carries an ease like rain falling on a spring morning.

It's calm and reassuring.

It settles me.

How can someone feel so settled in the most ambiguous places in life?

Perhaps, what feels unknown is about to be made known.

CHAPTER 34

Day 501

On this day I barely recognize myself. Much has changed, little has remained. In the space of what was, I find myself wondering about what will be. I've become more calm, more sure about these changes even if I can't see a guaranteed end in sight. I sit still more often, and fear the gradual shifts of life less. Something within me has been centered, something foundational has taken root. Subconsciously, I wonder how long this feeling will remain until another major shift comes and sweeps me off my feet. The thought is fleeting and moments later I catch myself feeling confident that if something comes to knock me off my feet, I will survive it, because I survived this.

The lessons in transition only come through change. When everything in life is constant, you don't get to see how capable you are of expansion. I'm learning there's so much of me to experience and I never would have crawled out of my hole if it weren't for transition. Like the seasons, something must die in order for other things to emerge.

I'm proud of what's emerged and proud of myself for being brave.

There's a subtle pulse I sense on the horizon. It sounds like a rested heartbeat. Like my life is about to change completely.

Life.

Some kind of new life is waiting for me. This place I've worked so hard to love myself in won't be home to me anymore. I don't know in what way things will shift but I sense a shift coming. Before Sam left, I had this similar feeling. Then, I felt like I was preparing for a funeral before I ever knew it was me that was going to be buried. Now, I feel this crescendo in life. Something is about to change and it will be beautiful, and it will be painless.

Sometimes a painless journey seems too good to be true but I believe that I will see goodness come into my life without it requiring pain. It's already happening. In some way, I think I'm being prepared for a new life without recognizing that all I've walked through is preparation for what will be. We think healing is simply to emerge from the past, but healing also brings us into our future. Without the transition, we cannot possibly acquire what is in the future.

Transition is the bridge we must cross over in our discovery for truth.

The sun is still out. It's a late September afternoon. I sit on the porch drinking a glass of wine while eating my favorite saucy pizza. I've been working on some material for a script based on a book I wrote two years ago. Writing centers me. I grabbed my phone and started doom scrolling for inspiration on a new character I'm developing. I saw a new message in my inbox from a beautiful stranger. His profile photo is what caught my attention. If you've ever felt like you knew someone deeply just by glancing at a photo, you'd know my heart skipped a few beats. He seemed supremely familiar, but I'd never seen him in my entire life. I opened the message, took a deep breath, and before reading its content, something within me said...

Ready or not, here it comes.

DEANNA LOREA is the author of *Unraveled, Undignified,* and her newest work, *Just Before Daybreak.* With a voice both tender and unflinching, Deanna writes for those standing in life's most honest pause—the space between fear and freedom, where starting over feels both impossible and inevitable.

Her work gives language to the in-between—those messy, sacred thresholds where identity shifts, truth rises, and healing begins. Whether drawn from the depths of experience or the spark of divine insight, Deanna invites readers to see themselves in her pages. Her stories don't offer easy answers—they offer permission. Permission to grieve, to release, to reclaim, and to begin again with boldness.

Now based in Los Angeles, Deanna has been deeply immersed in her writing practice, using this new chapter of life to explore what it means to move from fear into freedom, from silence into story. Her books have become trusted companions for those navigating major life transitions and seeking the courage to be fully seen.

*instagram.com/dahter_*
dahter.com

THOUGHT CATALOG Books

Thought Catalog Books® is a publishing imprint of Thought Catalog, a digital magazine for thoughtful storytelling, and is owned and operated by The Thought & Expression Co. Inc., an independent media group based in the United States of America. Founded in 2010, we are committed to helping people become better communicators and listeners to engender a more exciting, attentive, and imaginative world. The Thought Catalog Books imprint connects Thought Catalog's digital-native roots with our love of traditional book publishing. The books we publish are designed as beloved art pieces. We publish work we love. Pioneering an author-first and holistic approach to book publishing, Thought Catalog Books has created numerous best-selling print books, audiobooks, and eBooks translated into 40+ languages.

ThoughtCatalog.com | **Thoughtful Storytelling**

ShopCatalog.com | **Shop Books + Curated Products**

**More from
Thought Catalog Books**

Holding Space for the Sun
Jamal Cadoura

It Is All Equally Fragile
Alison Malee

The Unbearable BeautyPoems and Practices for Being Alive
Annabelle Blythe

Face Yourself. Look Within.
Adrian Michael

Eyes On The Road
Michell C. Clark

You're Overthinking It: Find Lifelong Love Being Your True Self
Sabrina Alexis Bendory

THOUGHT
CATALOG
Books

THOUGHTCATALOG.COM